A Note to Parents and Caregivers:

Read-it! Readers are for children who are just starting on the amazing road to reading. These beautiful books support both the acquisition of reading skills and the love of books.

The PURPLE LEVEL presents basic topics and objects using high frequency words and simple language patterns.

The RED LEVEL presents familiar topics using common words and repeating sentence patterns.

The BLUE LEVEL presents new ideas using a larger vocabulary and varied sentence structure.

The YELLOW LEVEL presents more challenging ideas, a broad vocabulary, and wide variety in sentence structure.

The GREEN LEVEL presents more complex ideas, an extended vocabulary range, and expanded language structures.

The ORANGE LEVEL presents a wide range of ideas and concepts using challenging vocabulary and complex language structures.

When sharing a book with your child, read in short stretches, pausing often to talk about the pictures. Have your child turn the pages and point to the pictures and familiar words. And be sure to reread favorite stories or parts of stories.

There is no right or wrong way to share books with children. Find time to read with your child, and pass on the legacy of literacy.

Adria F. Klein, Ph.D.
Professor Emeritus
California State University
San Bernardino, California

Editor: Jill Kalz
Designer: Joe Anderson
Page Production: Brandie E. Shoemaker
Creative Director: Keith Griffin
Editorial Director: Carol Jones
The illustrations in this book were created digitally.

Picture Window Books
5115 Excelsior Boulevard
Suite 232
Minneapolis, MN 55416
877-845-8392
www.picturewindowbooks.com

Printed in the United States of America.

Library of Congress Cataloging-in-Publication Data
Shaskan, Trisha Speed.
The three princesses / by Trisha Speed Shaskan ; illustrated by Burak Senturk.
p. cm. — (Read-it! readers)
Summary: Princesses Violet, Daisy, and Rose put on fancy clothes, prepare special
treats, and decorate their table before sitting down to a tea party.
ISBN-13: 978-1-4048-2422-5 (hardcover)
ISBN-10: 1-4048-2422-7 (hardcover)
[1. Princesses—Fiction. 2. Parties—Fiction.] I. Senturk, Burak, ill. II. Title. III. Series.
PZ7.S53242Thr 2006
[E]—dc22   2006003435

The Three Princesses

by Trisha Speed Shaskan
illustrated by Burak Senturk

Special thanks to our advisers for their expertise:

Adria F. Klein, Ph.D.
Professor Emeritus, California State University
San Bernardino, California

Susan Kesselring, M.A.
Literacy Educator
Rosemount–Apple Valley–Eagan (Minnesota) School District

PICTURE WINDOW BOOKS
Minneapolis, Minnesota

Princess Rose puts on a red dress and
a diamond necklace. Princess Daisy puts
on a yellow dress and a gold necklace.

Princess Violet puts on a purple dress and a pearl necklace.

The three princesses meet in the kitchen.

Princess Rose makes heart-shaped cookies.

Princess Daisy makes fancy sandwiches.
Princess Violet makes cherry muffins.

Princess Daisy puts a tablecloth on the table.
Princess Violet helps put the teapot on the stove.

Princess Violet brings teacups and saucers to the table.

Princess Rose brings plates and folded napkins.

Princess Rose sets a plate of heart-shaped cookies on the table.

Princess Daisy sets cream and sugar next to it.

Princess Violet carries a basket of muffins.

Princess Daisy carries a tray of fancy sandwiches.

Princess Rose picks flowers.

Princess Violet fills a vase with water.

Princess Violet sets the teapot
on the table.

Princess Rose, Princess Violet, and Princess Daisy all sit down.

The three princesses are having a tea party!

23

More *Read-it!* Readers

Bright pictures and fun stories help you practice your reading skills. Look for more books at your level.

Alex and Sarah 1-4048-1352-7
Alex and the Team Jersey 1-4048-1024-2
Alex and Toolie 1-4048-1027-7
Another Pet 1-4048-2404-9
Felicio's Incredible Invention 1-4048-1030-7
Izzie's Idea 1-4048-0644-X
Joe's Day at Rumble's Cave Hotel 1-4048-1339-X
Naughty Nancy 1-4048-0558-3
Parents Do the Weirdest Things! 1-4048-1031-5
The Princess and the Frog 1-4048-0562-1
The Princess and the Tower 1-4048-1184-2
Rumble Meets Harry Hippo 1-4048-1338-1
Rumble Meets Lucas Lizard 1-4048-1334-9
Rumble Meets Randy Rabbit 1-4048-1337-3
Rumble Meets Shelby Spider 1-4048-1286-5
Rumble Meets Todd Toad 1-4048-1340-3
Rumble Meets Vikki Viper 1-4048-1342-X
Rumble's Famous Granny 1-4048-1336-5
Rumble the Dragon's Cave 1-4048-1353-5
The Truth About Hansel and Gretel 1-4048-0559-1
Willie the Whale 1-4048-0557-5

Looking for a specific title or level? A complete list of *Read-it!* Readers is available on our Web site:
www.picturewindowbooks.com